Heads or Tails?

Bernadette Kelly

Raintree is an imprint of Capstone Global Library Limited,
a company incorporated in England and Wales having its
registered office at 7 Pilgrim Street, London, EC4V 6LB –
Registered company number: 6695582

To contact Raintree, please phone 0845 6044371, fax +44 (0)1865 312263,
or email myorders@raintreepublishers.co.uk.

First published in Australia by Black Dog Books in 2006
Copyright © Bernadette Kelly 2006
First published in the United Kingdom in 2014
The moral rights of the proprietor have been asserted.

Editor: Diyan Leake
Art Director: Kay Fraser
Graphic Designer: Emily Harris
Production Specialist: Michelle Biedscheid
Originated by Capstone Global Library Ltd
Printed and bound in China

Main cover photograph reproduced with permission
of Shutterstock (© Erik Lam). Background image reproduced with
permission of Shutterstock (© Ozerov Alexander).

ISBN 978 1 406 26671 9
17 16 15 14 13
10 9 8 7 6 5 4 3 2 1

British Library Cataloguing in Publication Data
A full catalogue record for this book is available from the British Library.

Heads or Tails?

Bernadette Kelly

Breathing in the scent of horses, I tossed a final forkful of soiled straw into a wheelbarrow. Then I fluffed up the remaining thick layer of clean, sweet-smelling straw on the stable floor.

I stood the pitchfork up against the stable wall and cast a satisfied eye over the stall. It was definitely up to Erica's standards.

I could hear Erica shouting directions to a rider in the indoor arena. I didn't know who it was, but I had mixed feelings. On one hand, I felt sorry for the poor rider who was being yelled at. But at the same time, I couldn't help feeling a little bit jealous.

Erica demanded hard work from her riders, but I knew it helped them become better. Erica had certainly helped improve my riding skills. I wished I could take lessons from her.

Once I had finished cleaning the stalls, I headed to a small room to mix up the evening feeds. Large bins, labelled with words like *oats*, *barley*, and *molasses*, lined the walls. I picked up a pile of plastic buckets stacked neatly in a corner. After lining the buckets up in two rows, I looked up at the wall.

"Hmm, what's on the menu for today?" I wondered aloud.

A large whiteboard showed a hand-drawn chart listing every horse's name, along with the exact mixture and measure of the feed for each horse. I used this to double-check the amounts as I scooped feed into separate buckets.

When I had first started working at the stables, Erica had always mixed the feeds herself. Some of the horses were extremely valuable and Erica wasn't taking any chances leaving the feeding to a new employee.

As I learned more about the stables, however, Erica started to give me more responsibilities. Now I was in charge of many tasks that would have once seemed impossible.

I could hardly imagine it now, but I'd once been a city girl whose only contact with horses was in the pages of books and magazines.

That was before my parents and I moved to Ridgeview.

When I first moved to Ridgeview, I felt like I'd never fit in. Then one of my new neighbours gave me a horse, and I joined the local riding club. The riding club was where I'd first met Erica, who was also the club's regular dressage instructor. I'd also met a whole new set of friends.

I finished mixing the last feed and walked out of the feed room. I took each bucket to a stall, where I tipped the feeds into the individual bins each horse ate from. The scent of molasses and the pleasant, grassy smell of the hay crept into my nose.

When I was finished distributing the feeds, it was time to bring the horses in from outside. The horses were creatures of habit. I knew they would be happy to follow the daily routine and bed down for the night – especially with the feeds waiting for them.

Once, I had forgotten to put the feeds out before bringing the horses in. They had all made such a fuss, kicking the stable doors and neighing. Erica had only laughed, but I knew that I wouldn't keep my job unless I did things right.

That was the one and only time I forgot the feeds.

I grabbed a halter and lead, labelled with the name Jewel, from a hook on the wall. Then I headed outside.

"Come on, Jewel," I called as I walked out to the paddocks. "I've got something yummy for you."

I led Jewel, a gentle grey gelding, back into the stable block. I released him into his stall.

"Good job, boy," I said, patting him on the nose.

I grabbed another halter and lead and went back outside to collect the next horse. Most of the horses that were boarded at Erica's stables were well behaved and easy to handle, but I was amazed at how different they were from my own horse.

While Bobby had sturdy little legs and a cute face, these horses were tall, elegant, and regal. I didn't mind, though. At least Bobby was all mine.

By the time I was ready to collect the last horse, dusk had settled over the paddocks. *I'd better hurry*, I thought to myself. *Erica likes all the horses to be safely tucked away in their stalls before dark.*

I had left my favourite horse until last. I reached up and grabbed the halter and lead labelled "Finn" from the hook and made my way down past the now-empty paddocks to the end of the row.

Finn was a striking bay gelding. He had four white socks marking his legs and a long blaze that ran all the way down his face, drizzling into a patch of pink on the tip of his muzzle.

At sixteen hands high, Finn was the tallest horse that I had ever seen. He was as solidly built as Erica's brick stable block. As imposing as his size was, though, I wasn't afraid of Finn.

He was a gentle giant. He always moved slowly and carefully, and the look in his eyes made me feel that he would never hurt me on purpose.

I reached up between Finn's ears and applied a tiny bit of pressure to the space between them. Finn immediately lowered his head and allowed me to slip the halter on him. The move was a basic training trick that Erica taught to all of her horses.

"Come on, boy," I coaxed, leading Finn along the path to the stables.

I didn't notice that anything was wrong until I unclipped the halter at the stall door and allowed Finn to walk on in. I gasped in shock at what I saw.

Finn's beautiful black tail had been cut completely off just below the base of his tailbone. Instead of trailing thickly down to his fetlocks, the sad remains of Finn's tail barely measured three inches long. I stared in horror at the little bit of hair that was left.

Finn was not one of the horses Erica owned. His owners, Linda and Jason McElroy, were boarding him at Erica's stables. I was puzzled. Why would they have wanted to cut Finn's tail like that? How was he going to swat flies with the hair that was left?

Frowning, I pulled the door to Finn's stall closed and watched him dig into his dinner. He munched steadily, watching me with big, soulful eyes. I wondered what Finn was thinking. He hadn't been given a choice about whether to keep his tail or not, and it made me feel sad.

With a final scratch to Finn's ear and a murmured farewell, I went in search of my boss. I found Erica cleaning up in the outdoor riding arena.

"I'm leaving now," I called to Erica from the arena gate.

Erica glanced up from what she was doing and smiled.

"Thanks for your help today, Annie," she said in return. "Are all of the horses settled for the night?"

"All done," I replied. "I was surprised to see Finn's tail, though. Why did the McElroys cut it like that?"

"Cut it?" Erica repeated. She looked at me blankly. "What are you talking about?"

"Finn's tail," I told her. "It's been cut off, almost to the dock."

Erica's face turned pale. She dropped the rake she was holding and took off towards the stables. I ran after her.

I caught up with Erica at the door to Finn's stall. Finn was still busy eating. He didn't notice the troubled expression on Erica's face. With his back facing the aisle, it was easy to see how short his tail was.

Frowning, Erica turned to face me.

"Have you seen or heard anything unusual this afternoon?" Erica demanded. "Was anybody hanging around out by the paddocks today?"

I shook my head. "I didn't hear anything except your voice while you were giving a lesson," I replied anxiously.

Erica had turned back to Finn. She was staring in disbelief at his mutilated tail.

"The McElroys didn't do this, Annie," she said, with a deep sigh. "They wouldn't dream of doing anything like this to their horse."

I hesitated. "So who do you think…" My voice trailed off.

I was beginning to realize that something very bad had happened.

"Finn's tail was fine when I gave him hay at lunchtime," Erica said. "It must have happened when you were cleaning the stalls, and I was giving a lesson."

Erica turned away and began walking quickly up a narrow path that led behind the stables and on to the house.

"You'd better stick around, Annie," Erica called back to me as she walked away. "Finn's tail has been stolen. I'm going to call the police. They'll probably want to interview both of us."

Chapter Two

The next day, I stood with my friend Reese Moriarty at the Ridgeview High School lockers while other pupils milled around. The walls echoed with the slamming of metal locker doors as pupils hurried to collect their books.

We had just returned from our lunch break. Between mouthfuls of a turkey sandwich, I had told Reese all about the tail-cutting incident at Erica's stables.

Reese – and her mother – had first got me involved with horses when I moved to Ridgeview.

When I had arrived in town, I hadn't known anyone. (Except for my parents, of course, and that didn't count.)

I had met Reese and her horse, Jefferson, while I was out walking my dog, Jonesy. We might have just passed each other by if it hadn't been for Jonesy chasing Jefferson and making Reese angry.

It hadn't exactly been the best beginning for a friendship.

Then I found out that Reese lived next door to me. We both lived in the country, just a short distance from Ridgeview. The two properties had once been part of a much larger farm. From the road, it was hard to tell which was which.

Each of our houses had a long, tree-lined drive that hid the house from the road. Once, driving home late at night, my father had gone halfway up the Moriartys' drive before realizing he was going to the wrong house.

When Reese's mother discovered that I liked horses, she invited me to come to the riding club with Reese. I went, even though I didn't have a horse of my own. Reese was not very welcoming.

Then something amazing happened. A kind neighbour, Mrs Cameron, gave me her old horse, Bobby. I couldn't believe my luck, especially when my dad agreed – very reluctantly – that I could keep the horse.

Even though we'd had a shaky beginning, Reese and I had become good friends. We were in the same year at school, but more importantly, we shared a love for horses, and rode together all the time.

"I just can't believe that anyone would do something so horrible to a poor innocent horse!" I exclaimed.

"What I don't understand is why," said Reese. "Why would anyone need all that horse hair?"

I shrugged. "Maybe someone's making dolls or puppets or something and using the tail for hair," I suggested.

"Right!" said Reese, rolling her eyes. "Or maybe aliens landed and took the tail back with them to analyse life on Earth."

I frowned at my friend. "Okay, I guess that does sound pretty lame," I agreed. "But what could be worse than stealing poor Finn's tail right out from under him?"

"You mean from behind him," said Reese.

We both closed our locker doors and started walking to our next lesson.

"Ugh, maths!" I groaned. "Almost two whole hours of Mr Waltham droning on and on. It's torture!"

"You better not let your mum hear you talking about Mr Waltham like that," Reese warned.

My mother was a teacher at Ridgeview High. Luckily, she didn't teach any of my lessons. I was extremely grateful for that.

"Besides," Reese continued, "I have science, and that's worse than maths. We're supposed to be watching some boring movie about the way plants reproduce." Reese frowned. "How fascinating!" she mumbled sarcastically.

I laughed as I left Reese and walked to my classroom. The rest of the maths class was slowly wandering in, but there was no sign of Mr Waltham yet.

I chose a desk near the door. I dropped my maths book on the desk and sat down. I couldn't concentrate. An image of poor Finn without his beautiful tail kept popping into my head.

Maybe Erica will have some news by the time I get to the stables for work tonight, I thought. *The police might have found some clues. Maybe they've already caught the thief.*

I hoped that was true. I liked my job at the stables, and I liked the fact that Erica needed my help.

Erica had to cram in as many lessons from paying customers as she could get. In addition to the lessons, she was paid to exercise some of the boarded horses, and she had her own horses to ride. Erica was training Cadence, her young chestnut mare, for dressage. She was getting her ready for a competition in a couple of weeks.

I was paid for my job at the stables, but I enjoyed the work so much I would have done it for free. I was also proud of the fact that in a small way, I had helped with Cadence's training.

Not long after I first began working at the stables, Erica had wanted a calm, quiet horse to help give Cadence confidence when riding out. More than once, she had asked me to bring Bobby over, and we had ridden out on the bridle paths together.

I had been proud of the way Bobby had led the way, calming the skittish Cadence while Erica taught her road manners.

I smiled at the memory. It all seemed so long ago now.

"Annie! Annie Boyd, are you with us?" a loud voice said, interrupting my daydreaming.

I looked up to see Mr Waltham. His angry eyes frowned down on me from behind round, rimless glasses.

I nodded. "Um, of course," I replied. "Yes, Mr Waltham."

"Good," he said smugly. "Then you'll know I'm collecting the homework assignments from last week. You can hand it in now."

I quickly pulled out my maths folder to hand in my assignment. But when I opened it, my assignment was nowhere to be found.

I felt my face turning red. Mr Waltham waited. His fingers tapped impatiently on the desk. I frantically looked through my folder. I flipped through twice, but my assignment definitely wasn't there. Mr Waltham's stare drilled into me, making me shrink back into the seat.

"Well?" the teacher asked.

I felt the eyes of every other pupil in the room on me. Most of them looked sympathetic. Everyone had been yelled at by Mr Waltham at least once in this class.

"I ... I finished it, I really did," I said quickly. "I just don't have it here..."

I knew I'd finished the assignment. It had been hard, and I'd had to ask my mum for help. I had been in a hurry to get outside and ride Bobby, though. I had left the homework sitting on my desk. I'd meant to put it into my rucksack last night.

Obviously, I hadn't.

Mr Waltham pushed back a thin strand of hair behind his ear. He was almost totally bald, with just a few longish tufts growing above his ears. He also had a large curved nose. He kind of looked like a baby eagle that hadn't grown all its feathers yet.

"So?" he asked. "Where is it?"

"It's at home," I replied apologetically. "I forgot to bring it."

"Well, Annie, I'm very glad to hear that you did it," my teacher said.

I winced at the sarcastic tone of Mr Waltham's voice.

"However, since the homework was actually due today, I would have thought that today would be a good time to bring it to school and hand it in," he continued.

Mr Waltham glanced around at the rest of the class. Then he looked down at a pile of already-collected papers in his hand.

"Obviously, the rest of the class thought so, too," he added.

I felt my eyes fill with tears. I wasn't used to getting into trouble at school, and it felt terrible. I thought it was mean of Mr Waltham to embarrass me in front of the whole class.

Why should I sit here and let him bully me? I thought. *It's only homework, after all.* I blinked away the tears from my eyes and sat up taller.

"I'm sorry, Mr Waltham. I can bring it tomorrow," I offered. "I could drop it off in the teacher's lounge first thing in the morning."

"I'm sorry. That's not good enough," Mr Waltham said. "You can redo the assignment this afternoon after school, while you're serving detention for failing to hand in your homework on time. It shouldn't take you too long, since you've already done it once."

Mr Waltham returned to the front of the room and began the class.

I was furious. Not only was I going to be forced to do redo my homework, but I was supposed to be working at Erica's stables this afternoon. Erica needed me, and I would have no choice but to let my boss down.

Stupid maths, I thought.

Chapter Three

I scanned row after row of glossy magazine covers at the Ridgeview bookshop. *Someone must buy all these magazines*, I thought. There were just so many. There were magazines about knitting and needlework, motorbikes and cars. There were computer magazines, fashion magazines, and interior design magazines.

I found the section I was looking for. The horse magazines were displayed right next to alpacas and sheep, which I thought was absolutely ridiculous.

Don't the owners of this shop know that horses have absolutely nothing in common with stupid sheep? I thought.

It was bad enough that Bobby had to share his paddock with the six sheep that belonged to my father. I didn't know much about alpacas, but they could have been sheep with long necks for all I cared.

I was trying to decide which horse magazine was worth spending part of my hard-earned money on. I'd narrowed it down to either the one with the stunning Arab stallion on the cover or the one with the article about the newest saddles available.

Then a conversation on the other side of the magazine display caught my attention.

"Did you hear about what happened to Miranda Jacobs's broodmare?" a dark-haired woman, wearing faded jeans and riding boots, said to an older man.

The word *broodmare* was enough to grab my attention. My radar was on high alert for anything to do with horses.

"Miranda Jacobs? I didn't know she had a broodmare," said the man.

"Well, someone came in overnight and cut the mare's tail right off," the woman went on. "Poor Miranda was devastated. That old mare was a top show horse in her day. I suppose it's just lucky that she's retired now. Otherwise it would have halted her career for a while. You know it takes a couple of years for a full tail to grow back properly."

"I've never heard of such a thing," said the man.

"Well, that's the third one I've heard of," the woman said. "If the police don't catch the culprit soon, we'll have a town full of bare-bottomed horses."

The old man snorted with amusement, but I was horrified. Who would do such a thing? I took my magazine up to the counter.

"That'll be three pounds fifty," said the cashier.

I practically threw the money on to the counter and hurried out of the shop. I needed to call Reese, but I also needed to get to Erica's. It wasn't my usual day to work, but I was making up time after my maths detention.

The conversation I'd overheard at the bookshop had worried me. Bobby had been fine when I'd left for school, but who knew what might have happened during the day? I fumbled in my pocket and pulled out my phone. I called Reese. It only rang a few times.

"Hi," answered Reese cheerily. "Aren't you supposed to be at work?"

"I'm on my way," I replied. "But I need a favour."

"Sure," Reese said. "What's up?"

"I just heard about another tail-cutting incident," I told her.

I heard Reese let out a shocked gasp through the receiver. "You're kidding!" Reese said. "Who?"

"The horse belonged to someone named Miranda Jacobs," I said. "The point is, our horses could be next. I have to go to work, but would you mind just checking on Bobby for me? My parents won't be home for a while, and I'd just feel better if I knew he was okay..."

My voice trailed off. The thought of Bobby losing his beautiful russet tail was almost too much for me.

"I'm already on my way," said Reese. "I just have to check on Jefferson first. Then I'll call you back."

I'm probably worried about nothing, I thought as Reese hung up. But what if someone did have an eye on Bobby's tail? And if they did, how on earth would I be able to stop them?

Reese called back just as I was arriving at the stables.

"They're both fine," Reese assured me.

I let out a huge sigh of relief. Thank goodness Bobby was okay.

"Thanks, Reese," I said gratefully. "You're a lifesaver."

Reese promised to keep an eye out for anything suspicious at my house until somebody made it home.

"I'll be your very own private eye," Reese joked. "I have very cheap rates."

I passed the small office near the stables. The office window looked out on to the dirt riding arena. I noticed that someone was riding in the arena, probably warming up for a lesson. Erica was in her office talking on the phone in a low voice.

Erica's expression was serious, and I wondered who my boss was talking to. I unhooked a pitchfork from its peg on the wall and began to clean the stalls.

Later that afternoon, I heard the sound of a horse's hooves thumping on to the ramp of a horse trailer. A car engine started and drove away. *That was the rider leaving*, I thought. *Erica's lesson must be over.*

Silence fell over the stables. Except for the occasional snort from one of the horses out in the paddocks, it was incredibly quiet.

Normally, Erica would poke her head inside the stable door, just to say hello and make sure that things were going okay. But not tonight.

She must have gone up to the house, I thought to myself.

I had wanted to ask if Erica had heard back from the police. I went outside to give Finn some attention, but when I got there, I discovered that he was missing from his paddock.

Finn's halter and lead, normally hanging from the gate for easy access, were also missing. *What's happened to poor Finn now?* I wondered.

I finished all my jobs and made my way up a narrow, weedy path to Erica's house.

Through one of the kitchen windows, I could see Erica sitting at a table. It was completely covered with books and papers. On top of those perched a couple of tilting coffee cups, a crumb-covered plate, and a box of tissues. There was even an old lead rope dangling from one corner.

Erica was slumped forward. One elbow rested on a book; the other nudged the side of the plate. She stared into space, looking worried.

I watched through the glass. To me, Erica had always seemed so focused. Busy and capable. It was alarming to see her sitting in that kitchen looking helpless, scared, and so obviously unhappy.

I felt like a spy. I tapped lightly on the door. I didn't want to bother Erica, but I just had to know what was going on.

Chapter Four

Erica opened the door and stared blankly at me for a moment.

"Annie," Erica said. She seemed confused. "You're finished already?"

I glanced down at my watch. It was almost six o'clock, the same time I always finished.

Erica turned to check the clock on the wall behind her and laughed. "Sorry," she said. "I'm just a little … tired. If you've fed all the horses I think I might have an early night. Do me a favour and lock up the stables before you go, okay, Annie?"

That made me even more worried. Every evening, the last thing Erica did was walk around checking on the horses. Even though she trusted me, Erica never let me be the one to lock up.

"Is everything okay?" I asked tentatively. "Are you… Is everything all right?"

"Oh, sure. Everything's fine," Erica answered quickly. Then, suddenly, her face crumpled as she burst into tears.

I guided Erica to a kitchen chair and handed her a tissue. I sat down in the chair across from her as she dabbed at her eyes.

Erica looked at my worried face and tried to smile. "It's okay, Annie. I'm just tired," she reassured me. "Nothing a good night's sleep won't fix."

But I wasn't fooled.

"Please, Erica," I begged. "Tell me what's wrong. Did another horse have its tail cut off? Have the police found anything yet? And where's Finn? He wasn't in his paddock."

Erica shook her head. "The horses are all fine. I'm afraid the police have no idea who would do such a horrible thing. Unless we catch someone in the act, there's nothing they can do."

Erica stopped talking then. She clenched her fists, crushing the tissue in her hand.

I waited quietly, and then asked, "Where's Finn?"

"Finn's gone," she said. Her voice became brisk. "The McElroys came and took him this morning."

I gasped. "Wait a second. Do they blame you for what happened to Finn's tail?" I asked.

"I'm afraid they do," she said sadly. "He was at my stable when it happened. And word is starting to get around to the other owners. I've had people calling me all day. They want guarantees that their horses are safe here. If it happens again, I'll lose more horses. I can't afford to keep the stables open without boarding money coming in."

"But you look after your horses better than anyone!" I argued. "They can't hold you responsible for some horrible tail thief."

Erica reached across the table and touched my hand lightly. It was now her turn to comfort me.

"It's not your problem," she said softly. "I'll work it out."

* * *

I checked on Bobby as soon as I got home. He was grazing happily. And his tail was fine.

I cupped Bobby's nose in my hands and stared into his brown oval eyes. Still chewing, the chestnut horse gazed back at me. Long strands of grass poked out of the sides of his mouth like whiskers.

"I wish you could talk," I said wistfully. "I bet you could help me figure out a way to help Erica."

Bobby, his grass mouthful finished, nibbled at my fingers hopefully. He was looking for a treat.

I scratched Bobby's ears. The horse lowered his head and pushed against my hand.

This person, this horrible tail thief, had to be stopped somehow. No horse in Ridgeview was safe until that happened.

* * *

The first thing I noticed as Reese and I rode into the riding club grounds the next day was the number of horses with tail bags attached to their blankets. In the past, the only person who would have used one was Jessica Coulson for her show horse, Ripple.

"Everybody's trying to find ways to protect their horses from the tail thief," said Reese. "It's not really a bad idea. If the horse is wearing a tail bag, the thief might think it's easier just to move on."

But I shook my head. "I don't see how it would make much difference. The tail bag is just attached to the blanket with a piece of Velcro. All the thief has to do is pull it off or even just cut through the fabric," I said.

Reese sighed. "You're probably right," she admitted. "But you can't blame people for trying to protect their horses."

I nodded in agreement. "I guess you're right," I admitted.

All anyone talked about at gear check was the missing tails. As Reese and I joined the rest of the group, I was relieved to see that all the other horses – Austin Ryan's mare, Cruise, Matt Snyder's Appaloosa, Bullet, and of course,

Jessica's Ripple – were all looking like they were supposed to, tails included.

Unfortunately, the news wasn't all good.

"Mrs Mason found the tail cut off her harness horse last night," Matt told everyone right away. "She called my dad first thing this morning."

When Mrs Mason arrived at the arena for gear check, we all told her how sorry we were about what had happened.

"Well, they better not let me catch them," said Mrs Mason angrily. "You should all keep an eye out for strangers hanging around. And report anything suspicious to the police right away. Now, who's first?"

Our group had games and then dressage for the morning sessions. As we waited for games to start, Bobby tossed his head excitedly. Bobby loved games, and we were even pretty good at it – after a lot of practice.

At the start line, Bobby pranced in place while I held out my arm to grab the baton from Matt as he raced past me.

Not long ago, I would have been terrified by Bobby's behaviour. Lately, however, I enjoyed the challenge of sitting quietly in the saddle, allowing my body to relax no matter what Bobby was doing.

Erica was the instructor for dressage. I looked at her anxiously. I knew that she must still be worried about the future of her stables.

But Erica was her usual bossy self. She made the group work extra hard, and by lunchtime we were glad to dismount. We were happy to give ourselves, and our horses, a much-needed break.

The weather was too nice to sit inside. Instead, we queued up at the lunch shed to buy some food, then headed outside. Everyone settled on a square patch of grass underneath a large tree.

I ate my burger and listened to the conversation around me. With everything that had been happening, I didn't feel much like talking.

"Maybe someone is taking the tail hair to make wigs," said Austin.

Matt nodded thoughtfully. "It's possible, I guess," he said. "But wouldn't the hair be too coarse for a human wig?"

The talk of wigs made me think of Mr Waltham.

"My maths teacher needs a wig," I said, joining the conversation. "But I guess even Mr Waltham wouldn't want to go around wearing a horse's tail on his head."

"That might be an improvement," joked Reese.

"I'm getting Ripple ready for a show next month," said Jessica, changing the subject. "Last year I won the ribbon for Supreme Champion. Mum thinks I can get it again this year."

Reese cut in nastily. "Don't you mean you and Ripple? She is carrying you around, after all," she said.

Jessica shot Reese an irritated glance. "I have no idea where I'm going to put another ribbon," she continued. "My bedroom wall is already completely covered."

I wasn't really interested in the lunchtime chatter. With twenty minutes left before the afternoon sessions began, I rose to my feet and dusted the grass off my trousers.

"I think I'll just go check on the horses," I announced. Then I headed towards the paddocks.

It had occurred to me that a riding club was a perfect place for a tail thief to hang around. Bobby was in one of the yards, and I didn't want to take any chances.

Chapter Five

The following Friday afternoon, Reese and I were waiting for my mum to drive us both home.

My mother was often busy with meetings or other commitments after work. Most of the time, I waited for her in the library at school. That way, I had some time to finish up homework or research an assignment. Tonight, though, Reese had asked if she could get a ride home with us.

"Let's go to the café," Reese suggested. "I don't want to hang around school. We can flip a coin to decide who buys."

"Um, sure," I said.

Normally, I would have welcomed a treat at Coasters. Tonight, however, I just wanted to get home and check on Bobby.

Spending time away from him these days was agonizing. It was almost impossible to concentrate on my schoolwork or work at the stables. I kept imagining poor Bobby in danger.

We were the only customers in the café. We chose a table in a dim corner, right at the back of the shop. I found a coin in my pocket and flipped it into the air.

"Heads," I called.

Reese and I watched the coin rattle across the floor before coming to a halt.

"Tails," called Reese, smiling. "You're paying!"

I shrugged. Reese often paid, so I didn't mind buying this time.

A middle-aged woman, her dark hair tied back in an old-fashioned bun, appeared from behind the counter.

"Annie," the woman greeted me warmly. "And Reese, too."

We both smiled in return. "Hello, Mrs Cameron," we called in unison, and then laughed at ourselves.

Mrs Cameron fished a notebook and pen out of her shirt pocket and looked at us. "What can I get you girls?" she asked.

"Two hot chocolates, please," I said.

Mrs Cameron wrote down the order and returned to the other side of the counter to make the drinks. Mrs Cameron liked to chat, and she continued talking as she made our hot chocolate.

"So how's our Bobby?" Mrs Cameron asked, as she always did when she saw me.

I didn't mind at all. Mrs Cameron had once been Bobby's owner. As far as I was concerned, Mrs Cameron had saved me from a life of boredom in a new town.

"He's still eating apples whenever he gets the chance," I reported.

That made Mrs Cameron laugh. She returned to our table, carrying a mug of frothy hot chocolate in each hand.

I wondered if Mrs Cameron had heard about the tail cutter. It had been almost two weeks now since Finn had lost his tail. The thief was still out there somewhere.

The bell on the shop door jingled. I looked up to see a woman and a girl in the doorway. As they came inside the shop, I recognized Jessica Coulson and her mother.

Jessica carried a large plastic bag. Reese gave a low moan when she realized who it was.

"Oh great. It's the fashion sisters," Reese said rudely, under her breath.

Beneath the table, I kicked Reese's foot. "Be polite," I whispered, then giggled softly.

Reese had a point. Jessica and her mother were always dressed up in expensive clothes. As far as I could see, there was no reason to dress up in a town like Ridgeview. Nobody cared what people wore here.

Mrs Cameron looked at Reese and me but said nothing. She placed the mugs on the table and left to serve Mrs Coulson.

Jessica spotted us and walked over to our table.

"Hi, Jess," said Reese.

I managed to force back a grin. Reese knew Jessica hated having her name shortened. For once, Jessica didn't seem to notice. She took the one empty seat at the table and sat down.

"How come you're home so early?" I asked.

Jessica went to a private school that was more than an hour's drive away from Ridgeview. Her bus wouldn't normally be back in town at this time of day.

"And why aren't you wearing your school uniform?" demanded Reese.

Jessica ignored Reese and answered me instead. "Mum picked me up early. We had to do some shopping for the show," she explained proudly.

Jessica held up the plastic bag. It was packed full. Something glittery poked up from the bag's opening. It caught my eye.

"What do you have in there?" I asked, pointing to the bag.

Jessica was more than happy to show us her purchases. She pulled out a beautiful browband, the part of a bridle that sits across a horse's brow, just below the ears. I knew what it was, but I had never seen one like this before.

The browband had been totally wrapped in woven strips of rich velvet. The green and gold fabric was interlaced in a diamond pattern. Each end of the browband was finished off with a decorative rosette, and the whole thing was set with three rows of sparkling gems.

The effect was stunning. I could just imagine how wonderful the browband would look against Ripple's black face.

While Reese and I were admiring the browband, Jessica began pulling the rest of her purchases from the bag. Her mother called out to her from the restaurant door.

"Jessica, I'm going over to the bank," she said. "You can wait here with your friends, if you like."

Mrs Coulson walked out the door, but Jessica hardly seemed to notice. She was too busy holding up a new hunter green show jacket, with a white shirt and a gold tie, for Reese and me to admire.

"There's more, too," Jessica bragged. "We're having Ripple trimmed and clipped tomorrow, and I ordered a false tail for the show."

"A what?" I asked.

At first I thought I must have heard her wrong. But then I noticed Jessica looking at me like she thought I must have been hiding under a rock all my life to not know what she was talking about.

"You know – a false tail!" she explained. "Lots of people use them at shows. I must admit, Ripple is practically perfect, but her tail is a little thin. That's her only flaw."

I choked a little on my drink.

Ignoring me, Jessica continued, "I guess I should have known that you two wouldn't know what they are. Neither of your horses have Ripple's quality. I guess Jefferson does have a nice thick tail, though. Even Bobby's isn't too bad. I doubt that either of you would ever need to use a false tail on your horses."

"Jefferson does have a magnificent tail," Reese agreed. "But I do know what a false tail is. You know, you're not the only one with horse knowledge, Jessica."

I kept quiet. I had never heard of false tails for horses, but I wasn't about to admit that – especially to Jessica. I didn't need to give her anything else to use against me.

And what did Jessica mean with her comment about Bobby's tail not being too bad? I'd always loved his long russet-coloured tail. I thought it was beautiful.

Then I thought of something. Something Jessica had said had just clicked with me.

"That's it," I cried in amazement. "Someone is stealing horses' tails, and I'll bet that's why. They're using them to make false tails."

"How dare you suggest that I would buy my false tail from a thief!" Jessica said angrily. "My mother and I shop at Quentin's. They only sell the best quality. They would definitely not be selling stolen horse tails. That's ridiculous!"

"Probably not," I said. "But what if they don't know the tails are stolen?"

"That's right," Reese agreed. "And besides, I doubt the tail cutter would be dumb enough to try to sell the false tails around here."

Reese gulped down the last of the hot chocolate in her mug and stood up. She looked at her watch.

"Come on, Annie. Your mum will be outside in a couple of minutes. We'd better go wait for her. See ya later, Jess," said Reese. She dragged me out of the café.

I giggled. "You're so mean, Reese," I said as the door closed behind us. "She still had lots more to show us."

* * *

My mother had barely parked when I jumped out and ran off to check on Bobby. The sheep ignored me, but Bobby sauntered up to the gate, sniffing hopefully at my pockets for an apple.

"Sorry, no apple today," I told him. I looked through the pocket of my school uniform for something to give him. I pulled out a squished muesli bar.

I yelped as a claw suddenly poked through the fabric of my school uniform. I looked down to see Jonesy, my Jack Russell dog. He was gazing up at me with pleading eyes.

"Just a tiny bite, Jonesy," I told the little dog. "The rest is for Bobby."

I unfolded the already-opened wrapper, and broke off a small corner for Jonesy. I leaned down to feed it to him. Then I held out the rest of the bar to Bobby.

"Here," I said. "The wrapper says this muesli bar contains oats, and it's ninety-nine per cent fat free. What more could a healthy horse ask for?" I smiled.

Bobby took the treat in his lips. I watched it quickly disappear from view. Bobby crunched his way through the muesli bar in seconds. Then he threw up his head and curled his lips towards the sky. I wasn't sure if he liked the muesli bar or not.

"Thank goodness it's Friday," I continued saying to my horse. "I'm not working this weekend. Erica's brother is staying over at the stables. That means I have all weekend to spend with you." I scratched Bobby's nose.

Bobby flicked an ear forward and let out a deep, breathy sigh.

My mobile phone suddenly beeped loudly, interrupting the afternoon peace. It was a text message from Reese.

"Called Jake," the message read. "Got number of false tail seller. Should we call?"

Jake was the owner of Jake's Travelling Tack Shop. I was impressed with the way Reese was thinking. There might be a way we could trace the tails back to the thief. I wasted no time texting back.

"Can I come over?" I typed back and pressed the send button.

"C u soon," Reese replied within seconds.

I ran inside to change. I decided to leave Jonesy in the house with my mother. Reese wasn't too fond of my little Jack Russell dog. They'd got off to a bad start. It would probably just be easier for everyone if he stayed home.

When I got to Reese's house, I found her waiting for me outside. She was sitting on a two-seater swinging chair. A pen and notepad lay in front of her on a small table, along with two glasses of raspberry lemonade and a bowl full of crisps.

The chair swayed as I plopped down beside Reese. From there, I could look back across the paddock to Hillgrove on my right.

Bobby and the sheep were hungrily devouring grass. To my left, there were more paddocks and a distant cluster of buildings that made up downtown Ridgeview.

I scooped up a handful of crisps and began popping them, one by one, into my mouth. As I munched on the crisps, Reese explained what she'd learned.

"Jake said this lady makes up the tails when she gets orders from customers. Her name is Elizabeth Collier," she told me.

"Why don't we call her now?" I said.

Reese shrugged and handed me the notepad.

"My phone battery died," she said. "We have to use the phone inside or your phone."

Somehow I didn't think Reese's mum was going to be thrilled to learn we were trying to find the tail thief. Mrs Moriarty would probably tell us it was a job for the police and to stay out of it. At least I knew that's what my own mother would say.

"Who's going to call?" asked Reese.

"I'll toss you for it," I replied, pulling a coin out of my pocket. I chose heads and lost ... again.

I made a mental note to choose tails next time. Then I reached into my jeans pocket for my mobile phone. I glanced down at the number Reese had written on the notepad and bent my head to type it into my mobile. There was a long pause while we both waited for the call to be answered.

"Hello?" a woman's voice answered.

"Hello, is this Elizabeth?" I asked, using my most official-sounding phone voice. I wanted this woman to think I was serious about wanting to buy a false tail.

"That's me," the woman replied. "What can I do for you?"

"I was wondering if you could give me some prices for your false tails," I said.

"My prices start at a hundred and fifty

pounds," Elizabeth told me. "That's for a standard false tail. The price can go up from there. It depends on the length, thickness, and colour of the tail you want."

Reese was busy making funny faces at me trying to make me laugh. She crossed her eyes and stuck her tongue out at me, then puffed up her cheeks with air.

"Hmm, I see," I continued, as Elizabeth talked. I tried to ignore Reese. "Yes, I think that sounds like a reasonable price."

I shook my head at Reese, trying to signal to her to knock it off. "And are your false tails synthetic?"

"All of my false tails are made from real horse hair," Elizabeth replied. She sounded a little insulted. "It's one of the details I pride myself on. I would never sell a fake tail to one of my customers."

"Oh, real horse hair!" I exclaimed, pretending to be shocked. "You're kidding! Where on earth do you get that from?"

Reese rolled her eyes at my question. I could tell she thought I sounded silly. I continued to ignore her as Elizabeth spoke.

"Oh, I see… Okay… No, I didn't know that," I replied, suddenly feeling more serious.

"Is there anything else I can help you with?" Elizabeth asked. "Or would you like to go ahead and place an order?"

"Sorry, what did you say?" I asked. I turned away from Reese. "Would I like to place an order?"

Choking back giggles, Reese made a face at me. "Stop! Hang up!" she whispered.

My voice cracked slightly as I mumbled, "Ummm, well… I'll get back to you on that. I have to decide on a colour. Thanks for your help."

I hung up the phone quickly as Reese burst into laughter.

"A colour?" she said. "That was the best excuse you could come up with? Don't you remember what colour Bobby's tail is?"

"Reese, this is serious!" I exclaimed.

"You're right," Reese agreed, still trying to get her laughter under control. "But you should have heard yourself. You sounded like the biggest snob!"

In spite of myself, I couldn't help laughing aloud. I grinned and put on an exaggerated voice.

"Really, daaarling? You don't say," I said, fluttering my eyelashes dramatically. "How absolutely maaarrvellous."

"So what did she say?" asked Reese when we had both stopped laughing.

I sighed. "She said she gets all the hair for the false tails from old horses at auctions," I told Reese. "If nobody buys them, the tails are cut off."

Reese and I both grew serious at this piece of information. Reese shuddered.

"How sad for the poor horses that end up there," said Reese.

"I know, and how awful to think that old and unwanted horses have their tails cut off," I said.

"It's horrible, but that doesn't mean it's illegal," said Reese. "Well, that was a waste. I can't think of another way to find the tail thief. Can you?"

I shook my head. I had been so sure I was on to something with the false tail idea. Now it seemed like we were back at square one.

An image of Mr Waltham's balding head flashed into my mind.

No way, I thought quickly. *That's ridiculous. My maths teacher is not a tail thief.*

But even though I tried to dismiss it, the image wouldn't budge.

Chapter Seven

I left Reese's house and made my way back to Hillgrove. All around me, the signs of spring were beginning to appear. Trees that had been in bud just a few short weeks ago were suddenly bursting with flowers and new leaves. The grass in Bobby's paddock suddenly looked thicker and greener, and the evenings seemed to last longer. It was a great change from winter.

I looked up at the sky, wondering how much longer it would be light out. I headed straight for Bobby's paddock.

I didn't think I had enough time to go for a ride before dark. But if I hurried I could at least give Bobby a good grooming. Bobby's winter coat had started to fall out, and his whole body was covered in loose hair that needed to be brushed away.

Using a rubber currycomb, I rubbed energetically at Bobby's coat. Bobby seemed to enjoy being groomed. He stood patiently at the gate while I worked on him.

In just a few minutes, a cloud of swirling chestnut horse hair surrounded me. It clung to my jeans and T-shirt in a thick layer.

While I worked, I thought about the unique way nature kept a horse warm and cool throughout the changing seasons.

When the first signs of winter had appeared, Bobby's coat had started to thicken and lengthen. The thicker coat helped give him warm, all-over protection for the colder months.

Now, warm weather was approaching, and the days were getting longer again. In preparation for the summer months, Bobby was shedding the old hair.

Soon his thick coat would be replaced with short, fine hair that was soft and silky to the touch.

Bobby is so lucky, I thought while I worked. *It must be nice to have your own personal heating and cooling system.*

My phone buzzed loudly in my pocket. I put down the currycomb, spitting hairs from my mouth as I raised the phone to my ear. "Hello?" I said.

"Hi, Annie," a man's voice said. "It's Jake. From the tack shop."

I tried not to sound too surprised. I had met Jake once at Reese's, not long after I first got Bobby.

I had desperately wanted to buy some of Jake's tack. It had all been way too expensive for my budget, though. I'd had no choice but to settle for cheaper secondhand gear instead.

"Reese told me you're interested in buying a false tail," Jake continued.

"She did?" I asked, surprised. "I am? I mean, oh, yes, that's right."

I thought fast. Reese must have used me as an excuse to get the number for the false tail lady, I realized. But why was Jake calling me now?

"Well, I just got a call from someone who wanted to sell me some cheap tails," Jake was saying. "False tails are usually pretty expensive, so I thought you might be interested in these. I already have a supplier myself, but I don't mind passing the details on."

Jake coughed, sounding a little embarrassed. "I know you have a limited budget," he said.

Excitement rose inside me at this new lead. "That's right," I said. "Thanks so much for thinking of me."

Clutching the phone to my ear, I asked Jake to wait a moment. I raced inside to find some paper and a pen. I took down the name the person had given him – Terry's Tails – as well as a mobile phone number and a website address.

I thanked Jake again and hung up. This new information was exactly the break I needed. Maybe I could still figure out who was responsible for the stolen tails.

I hurried to finish grooming Bobby. Then I collected my grooming gear and said goodnight to my horse.

Back inside, my mother was preparing dinner in the kitchen. "Mum, I need to use the computer," I said, passing through the kitchen on my way to the study.

Mum stared at me. "You're covered in hair!" she exclaimed. "I can't put those clothes through the washing machine like that."

I blinked, looking sheepishly at my mother. "I can't help it," I said. "Bobby's shedding." I tried changing the subject. "The computer," I repeated. "Can I use it? I need to get online."

"If you need it for homework, you can," she said. "If it's working, that is. Your father was complaining that the internet was down again last night."

My mother shook her head as she turned back around. "But first take off those dirty clothes and take them outside to shake them off. Try and get as much hair off them as possible," she told me.

"Sure, Mum," I said. I figured that since I hadn't actually said I was using the internet for homework, it wasn't technically a lie.

In my room, I changed out of my hair-covered jeans and T-shirt. Then I took them outside to shake them off. When I finished, I tossed them into the laundry basket.

By the time I made it to the study to use the computer, my nerves had kicked in. I left the door open a crack. My hands shook as I typed in the website. I had the strongest feeling that I was really on to something.

The site was very basic. I found the phone number that Jake had given me, some photos of false tails, and an email address. I scrolled through the pictures. There were several rows of tails, all different colours and shades.

My gaze stopped at one of the photos on the screen. It was a black tail, particularly thick and long. I wasn't positive, but it could have been Finn's tail.

I stared at the photo. Plenty of horses had black tails. I knew a few pictures of tails on a website didn't prove anything. But the feeling wouldn't go away. I needed solid evidence that would point to the thief. And it had to be convincing.

I thought of Bobby and all of my friends' horses. Until this thief was caught, no horse was safe.

And what about poor Erica? I felt terrible for her. If another tail went missing from her stables, she might lose everything – her business and her home.

The police had already told Erica that the thief would have to be caught in the act. What if that never happened? What would she do?

I scrolled back up the page to the email address at the top. Something was bothering me about that name... Terry... Terence...

That was it! My mother had called Mr Waltham Terence. Terry was short for Terence.

I shuddered. What if my maths teacher turned out to be the tail thief after all?

There was something I could do. It was risky, but if I was careful … it could work. I clicked on the email link to begin a new message.

I can always delete this if I change my mind, I thought.

I started typing slowly. As the letters appeared on the computer screen, my message began to take shape.

Hi Terry,

I'm wondering if you can help me. I have a friend who needs a false tail for her horse, and I'm thinking about buying her one as a birthday present.

I stopped typing and thought about what to write next. My breathing had quickened. The muscles in my chest tightened. Determinedly, I typed on, adding what I hoped was a casual tone to the words. I wanted the seller to think I was just being friendly.

I've never needed a false tail before. My own horse is lucky enough to have a gorgeous thick tail, so this is all very new to me.

Anyway, I guess I need to send you a photo or something to try and match the tail with. Could you please contact me and let me know what type of info you need from me?

Sometimes our internet doesn't work, so you can contact me by post at 24 Pine Street, Ridgeview.

Thanks,

Annie Boyd

I read back my message. I immediately wondered what on earth I'd been thinking. This was way too risky. For starters, the email included my name and my address.

If I was right and this person from Terry's Tails was a thief, I might as well just cut Bobby's tail off myself!

This idea was beyond stupid, I thought.

I moved the mouse cursor to the top of the page, where it hovered over the delete button. *There's no way I should send this*, I thought. *It would be way too dangerous.*

Suddenly, I saw a movement at the door out of the corner of my eye. Jonesy. His dark little eyes found mine. In a split second, Jonesy raced across the room and leaped on to my lap. He knocked my hand sideways in the process.

"No!" I cried out, watching the computer screen as the mouse clicked.

Instead of the delete button, I had accidentally clicked the send button. I stared down at the dog in my lap.

"Jonesy," I whispered in horror. "What have we done?"

Chapter Eight

Dinner that night was awful. I kept leaving to run outside and check on Bobby.

"What on earth's the matter with you?" my father asked after the third time I left the table. "We're eating dinner, Annie."

I decided it was probably better to be as truthful as possible.

"Someone is going around cutting off horse's tails," I told my father. "And the police don't have any idea who's doing it."

My mother looked up sharply. "Oh, Annie," she said with concern. "That's awful. You must be so worried about Bobby."

I nodded. The stress of the past couple of days was finally getting to me. My mother's sympathy made me feel like crying.

I thought about telling my parents about the email I'd accidentally sent. I stopped myself, though. I didn't think my dad would be quite so understanding – especially if he found out I had sent my name and home address to a total stranger.

Unlike my mother, my dad made light of my news. "It's probably just some kid," he said dismissively. "There's nothing to be worried about. And besides, there's not much point running outside every five minutes. It's not like anybody would bother sneaking around in the dark just to cut off a horse's tail. What a waste of time."

I felt sick with worry. I looked down to avoid my father's gaze as I took a bite of lasagna. It looked delicious, but I hardly tasted it. I might as well have been chewing on straw.

* * *

I woke up really early the following morning. The first thing I did was run outside to make sure that Bobby still had a tail. I breathed a sigh of relief when I saw that his beautiful tail was still in one piece.

Then I quickly ran inside to eat a light breakfast of toast and orange juice before heading back out to saddle up.

I still didn't have a clue what to do about the email. I'd been making a mental list of all the possible consequences that could come of sending that one dumb message.

Things weren't looking very good. The list kept growing.

I was hoping a quiet ride through the nearby country park would give me some time to think of a way out of the mess I'd created.

It had been quite a while since I had taken Bobby out for a ride by myself. Usually Reese came with me on Jefferson. After what had happened last night, though, I wasn't quite ready to face Reese. I couldn't tell her what I'd done.

Reese would know that something was wrong. I might be able to fool my parents, but Reese was harder to trick.

I could imagine exactly what Reese would say when I told her. "What have you done, Annie?" she would exclaim. "We have to tell our parents."

Which is exactly what I wasn't prepared to do.

The sun was shining and the day was beginning to warm up, but there was still a faint breeze in the air. I trotted Bobby along the gravel track leading to the country park.

At the end of long drives, houses nestled behind the leafy bushes and towering trees. They looked safe, but a tail thief could easily find his way behind the bushes and fences.

As I rode farther away from Hillgrove, the houses got farther apart. Slowing to a walk, I turned Bobby down a narrow dirt path.

Dim shade surrounded Bobby and me as we entered the forest. Almost immediately, shouting from behind me broke the morning stillness. Someone was calling my name.

"Annie, wait up," a boy's voice hollered.

I drew Bobby to a halt and twisted in the saddle to look behind me. Matt Snyder and his older sister, Laura, were riding towards me on their horses.

Just like every time I saw them together, I was struck by the differences between Matt and his sister.

Matt was wearing a pair of jodhpurs with a hole in the knee and a sweater that looked forty years old. It was dark blue but covered with dried splatters of white paint.

He looked like he'd dug through a bag of rags and thrown on whatever came out first. Matt's helmet and boots were the only things he was wearing that looked like they weren't antiques.

The Snyder family had been involved with horses and riding for many years. I knew Matt's parents would always make sure that his safety equipment was up to date. They would never allow him to ride with dangerous gear.

I noticed that Matt's horse, Bullet, looked clean and well groomed, even though his rider wasn't.

Laura, on the other hand, had her hair tied back in a neat ponytail. She was dressed in a white T-shirt with a clean, bright yellow riding vest over it.

The two were as different as the colours of their horses. Bullet was a spotted Appaloosa, while Laura's horse, Sunny, was a buckskin. He had a coat of bronze gold, with black mane and tail. The lower halves of his legs, near his hooves, were marked with black "points," similar to socks.

How can these two actually be brother and sister? I wondered.

"Hey, do you want some company?" asked Matt.

On this particular day, I wished I could just tell them, "No thanks." But, of course, I didn't. Instead, I nodded, trying to look excited. My face must have given me away, though.

"Hey, is something wrong?" asked Laura with concern.

Matt, too, was staring at me with a slightly alarmed expression. "Yeah, Annie," he said. "You look like something terrible has happened."

That did it for me. Matt was right. Something terrible had happened. And I needed to tell someone.

I took a deep breath and started to explain. There, on horseback in the middle of a bridle path, shaded by the tree branches overhead, I blurted out the whole story to Matt and his sister. By the time I finished, I was sobbing.

Matt gathered up his reins in his hands. I could see how uncomfortable he was at the sight of my tears. He looked as if he was thinking about whether to turn Bullet and bolt for home, but he didn't.

Between gulping breaths of air, I managed to finish telling them what had happened the night before.

"I … just … don't … know … what … to do," I gasped. "I've made a terrible mistake, and if Bobby's tail is cut off it'll be all my fault."

Laura dismounted from Sunny. She found a tissue in her riding vest pocket and handed it to me. Gradually, my sobs slowed. I wiped Laura's tissue across my cheeks to dry up the tears.

Finally, Matt spoke up. "Well, we'll just have to catch this creep in the act," he said. "That was why you wrote the email in the first place, wasn't it? So why don't we just carry out your plan?"

I stared at Matt. A tiny gleam of hope began to stir inside me. Maybe...

"You'll help me?" I asked gratefully.

"Sure," said Matt. "You're not the only one who's worried, you know. None of us want to see another tail go missing."

Matt turned around and looked at Bullet's tail. "Not that I have to worry much," he said. "Bullet's tail is pretty thin. He's a typical Appaloosa. I think he must have been last in the queue when tails were handed out."

"I'll help, too," Laura added. "But Annie, how were you planning to do it? Catch this guy, I mean."

"How do you know it's a guy?" Matt asked. "It could just as easily be a girl doing this, you know."

"I just can't imagine any girl being heartless enough to cut off some poor horse's tail," said Laura.

"Thanks a lot," said Matt. "So now you're saying I'm heartless because I'm a boy?"

I could see an argument brewing. "It doesn't matter who it is," I interrupted quickly. "The point is, we need to catch them. Now that I sent that stupid email, there's a good chance they could come around here soon … maybe even tonight."

Matt and Laura stopped arguing and turned their attention back to me.

"We could camp out at your house tonight," Matt suggested. "The thief will be looking for your place, so it's obvious that Bobby's the most likely victim."

I flinched at the idea of Bobby being a victim, but Matt was right.

"I haven't told my parents," I confessed. "Or anyone else, for that matter."

Both Matt and Laura agreed that it was probably better to keep our plans between the three of us. There was no point in sending everyone else into a panic.

"We'll come to your place later this afternoon," said Matt. "And we'll bring our tent and sleeping bags. Bobby and the sheep won't be the only ones sleeping under the stars at Hillgrove tonight."

Laura looked at me sympathetically. "Don't worry, Annie. We'll get him," she said.

I kept quiet about Mr Waltham being my prime suspect. I knew it was a silly idea. A local high school teacher could not be a horse-tail thief.

Or could he?

Chapter Nine

Matt and Laura arrived at my house just before dark with their father. Mr Snyder just happened to be my dad's boss. He was also the games instructor at the riding club.

He stood with my parents watching as Matt, Laura, and I set up our tent just outside Bobby's paddock.

"I have to say," said Mr Snyder with enthusiasm, "it's great to see the kids spending time together. Camping out! What a great idea."

I shot a warning glance at Matt and Laura. I had told my parents that I had met up with the Snyder kids while out riding, and we had decided to camp out for the night at Hillgrove.

"In the morning they can all come inside for a home-cooked breakfast," my dad said.

My mother was a little less sure about the whole idea. "Don't you think the nights are still a little cold for this kind of thing?" she asked. Both dads shook their heads.

"They've all got good warm sleeping bags inside that tent," my dad told her. "Besides, it'll toughen them up. Kids these days don't rough it enough."

"That's right," Mr Snyder chimed in. "It's all about computers and those video games. They're always on their mobile phones or listening to those tiny little music machines stuck to their ears." I knew that Mr Snyder was heavily into outdoor life.

"They're called MP3 players, Dad," Laura said, rolling her eyes at her dad.

I was secretly pleased that all of the adults liked the camping idea. Having their permission, for this at least, meant there was one less thing for me to feel guilty about.

I kept glancing nervously across the paddock to Reese's place. If Reese saw the tent and sleeping bags, she'd come over to ask what was going on.

There was a large Japanese maple tree that would block part of Reese's view, but at this time of the year it was only just beginning to grow leaves after being bare all winter. Still, I felt uncomfortable about not telling my friend the truth.

Mr Snyder said goodbye and left, promising to return in the morning to pick up Matt and Laura. A few moments later, my father returned to the house.

My mother glanced at the overcast sky. "Come inside and sleep on the living room floor if it rains," she said. Then she went inside, too.

Matt, Laura, and I climbed inside the tent. The moon was three-quarters full, and it gave off enough light for us to be able to see each other and the shadows of Bobby and the sheep.

It was a mild night, warmer than it could have been at that time of year. I was grateful for that. At least we wouldn't be freezing while we kept an eye out for the thief.

After an hour or so of hanging out, Matt volunteered to take the first watch while Laura and I snuggled into our sleeping bags. Then we would swap.

Matt fiddled with his watch. He set an alarm for when it was time for me to take over.

"I'll wake you up in a couple of hours," he told me.

Matt sat upright near the open door of the tent with his sleeping bag wrapped around him for warmth.

"Wake us up sooner if you see anything suspicious," said Laura with a yawn.

Laura lowered her head on to her pillow, rolled over on to her side, and was instantly asleep. It took me longer.

I lay there listening to the night. I could hear the soft but rhythmic tearing sound of the animals grabbing at the grass before pulling it free. I could also hear the steady sound of Matt's breathing nearby as he kept watch.

I felt really grateful for Matt and Laura. This morning, I had been desperate. I'd been alone and in way over my head.

Tonight, though, I had the help of my friends. We were following a clear plan of action, and things didn't seem as terrible as they had the night before. Maybe everything would work out after all.

If determination has anything to do with it, we're definitely going to catch this thief, I thought. Then I wondered, *Is it really possible that Mr Waltham could be the tail thief?*

With that disturbing thought, I finally drifted off to sleep.

* * *

The next thing I knew, a blinding shaft of sunlight was piercing through the tent. I blinked and turned my head into my pillow sleepily. Then I sat straight upright as I realized what the sunlight meant.

I had slept through the night. Matt hadn't woken me when it was my turn to act as the lookout.

Laura lay beside me, still sound asleep. I struggled out of my sleeping bag and crawled out of the tent. I expected to see Matt, but he was nowhere to be seen.

Bobby was standing at the gate, his head over the fence. When I suddenly appeared from inside the tent, the horse leapt back, startled.

"Whoa boy," I said gently. "It's only me." I cast a nervous glance at Bobby's behind. But I breathed a relieved sigh when I saw his russet-coloured tail.

My bare feet curled in shock as they made contact with wet, dewy grass. I reached for my shoes and hurriedly put them on. Inside the tent, I heard Laura stir.

"What time is it?" Laura's sleepy voice asked.

"I don't know, but we slept right through the night. Matt didn't wake us up," I replied.

"Typical," said Laura. "Oh no. Is everything okay with Bobby?"

"He's all right," I replied. "Are you coming in for breakfast?"

Laura stretched and blinked. "You go," she said sleepily. "I'll be in soon."

I left Laura and made my way into the house. My parents and Matt were sitting around the kitchen table, already eating a hearty breakfast of crispy bacon and scrambled eggs.

"Good morning," my dad said in greeting. He seemed much more cheerful than usual.

I wondered if Matt was the reason. My father was usually the only male in our house. He didn't often have the chance to hang out with another guy over breakfast.

Matt looked at me apologetically.

"What happened?" I asked, glaring at him angrily. "You were supposed to wake Laura and me up."

Matt shot me a warning glance, but it was too late. Both my parents looked up at me.

"Wake you up for what?" asked my father, just as Laura walked in the back door. "Annie, what's going on here?"

Matt and Laura's faces both turned red. I could feel my own face getting hot, too. I stared from one parent to the other. I didn't know what to say.

Now I'd really messed up.

By the time I finished explaining the whole story to my mum and dad, our breakfast was cold.

"But why didn't you come to us sooner?" my mother wanted to know. "For all we know, the three of you could have been in serious danger, Annie."

Mum was upset. But Dad was angry. "I can't believe you gave out our address in the email," he snapped at me.

"I'm really sorry, Dad," I said. "I was just trying to keep any more horses from having their tails stolen." Even as I said the words, I knew my excuse sounded weak.

My father wasn't finished. "And now you've dragged Matthew and Laura into it," he fumed. "What am I supposed to tell their father?"

Matt spoke up for the first time. "It's not all Annie's fault, Mr Boyd," he said. "We offered to help."

But my dad was not in a forgiving mood. In fact, I'd never seen him so angry. He ignored Matt and turned back to me. "Your mother is right," he said. "This thief could be dangerous, and three kids are no match for a criminal. I'm calling the police about this. There won't be any more camping."

My father pointed at Matt and Laura. "Annie, you owe these two an apology," he said. "And I'm going to have to punish you for putting everyone in such a dangerous situation. No riding for two weeks!"

I gasped. No riding! My father might as well have cut off my hand. "That's not fair!" I exclaimed. "It's not like anything even happened last night. We're all fine."

"That's enough, young lady," my father snapped. "We're done discussing this."

My mother insisted on making a fresh batch of bacon and eggs, but no one felt like eating. After breakfast, Matt, Laura, and I went outside to roll up our sleeping bags. Nobody said anything.

Mr Snyder came to pick up Matt and Laura shortly after breakfast. Before they left, he and my father had a long conversation. Neither of them was smiling.

Matt, Laura, and I couldn't hear what they were saying, but I could tell that my father was filling Mr Snyder in on what had happened last night. I tried to apologize to my friends for the trouble I'd caused.

"It's not your fault, it's mine," said Matt, shaking his head. "If I hadn't fallen asleep on duty…"

"But I should never have dragged you guys into it," I insisted.

"Look, there's no point in anyone taking the blame," Laura said forcefully. "It's out of our hands now. Mr Boyd is going to call the police, and all of our parents will be watching us like hawks for a while. We might as well accept the fact that there's nothing else we can do for now."

* * *

Later that day, two police officers – a large, older woman in a blue uniform and a thin, younger man with a startled expression – arrived to question me.

My father had told them everything, but they wanted me to give them my own version of events.

"Annie Boyd? Didn't I speak to you at Erica's stables the other day?" asked the young man.

I nodded. "That was me," I said. Then I told them the whole story.

"Did you get a reply from the website?" asked the female officer, taking notes in her notepad.

I shook my head.

The police officers gave me a harsh lecture about the dangers of taking the law into my own hands. Then they promised to look into Terry's Tails and see what they could come up with.

"We'll have a car do a regular patrol of the area, just in case," the policewoman assured us. "Just leave it to us, Annie. Promise me you won't try to catch this person yourself."

I nodded. I figured the police were right. At least now they had a possible lead.

After they left, I realized I had forgotten to mention my fears about Mr Waltham.

* * *

For the first time in ages, I went to bed that Sunday night feeling like I might get a good night's sleep. Knowing the police were watching the area helped a lot.

If the tail thief was lurking around, the police would see him. With any luck, he'd be caught before any more horses lost their tails.

I was still mad about my father's punishment, though. How was I going to survive two whole weeks without riding Bobby?

At least I knew that my punishment would be over before the next riding club event. That made me feel somewhat better.

I loved everything about the riding club, from show jumping to games and dressage. The days I spent at the riding club once a month gave me a chance to ride with my friends. More importantly, they gave me the chance to get a full day of riding instruction.

In the middle of the night, I was awoken by the sound of a low growl. It came from just outside my bedroom window.

Jonesy had an outside kennel with a covered run. It was my job to lock him in there at night. But that night, I'd forgotten.

A sharp, very loud bark made me hurry. If Jonesy woke my parents up with his barking, I'd be in trouble again.

I jumped up and opened the window. Jonesy was standing next to the Japanese maple tree in our yard. His ears and eyes were focused on something across the paddock, in the direction of Reese's place.

It's probably just a rabbit or something, I thought.

"Shush!" I told the dog. "I'm coming out to get you."

The little Jack Russell flicked his ear, but he didn't turn his head. He stayed focused on whatever was across the field.

I fumbled around my room, slipping my feet into slippers and pulling a dressing gown on over my pyjamas. Then I padded quietly down the hall and out the back door.

The moonlight was even brighter than it had been the night before. I could see everything clearly – even if it was in shades of grey instead of colour. I made my way outside to find my dog.

"Jonesy," I called in a loud whisper. "Come on, boy, let's go."

Still nothing happened. "Jonesy, get over here now!" I snapped.

Sighing loudly, I walked around the side of the house. I found Jonesy in the same place outside my window. He hadn't moved. He was still staring at something across the paddock.

Curious, I tried to see what Jonesy was looking at. I had been about to scoop the little dog into my arms, but a flicker of movement on the road outside Reese's house suddenly grabbed my attention.

"What is it, boy?" I asked quietly.

There was something there. Whatever it was, it was hidden by a stand of pine trees on the roadside. I couldn't see a thing.

Just then, I heard the thud of a car door closing. I hadn't seen any headlights, but someone had pulled up outside Reese's house.

The Moriartys' house was in darkness.

Wouldn't someone coming home this late at night have the headlights on? I wondered. *And why are they parking out front instead of going down the drive?*

My heart pounded in my chest. I focused my eyes on the trees. Yes, there was definitely a car over there. And a moving shadow, a human figure, was climbing through the fence. The shadow started running across Reese's front yard.

My eyes scanned the road, looking for lights. I was shaking.

Where was the patrol car the police had promised?

I was suddenly sure that the shadowy figure was the tail thief. And he had gone to the wrong house!

Chapter Eleven

Jonesy growled again. I grabbed him around the middle and picked him up, clamping my hand around his muzzle.

There was no time to waste. I had to stop the tail thief before he found Jefferson.

What if Jonesy made a noise and gave away my presence? If I put him in his kennel, he might still bark and alert the thief.

With the dog in my arms, I ran around to the laundry room door. Jonesy whined as I pushed him inside the laundry room. I quickly closed the door before he could get out again.

"Sorry, boy," I muttered.

I ran to my bedroom, grabbed my mobile, and then ran towards Reese's house. I would keep an eye on the thief while calling the police.

I knew that if I could see the thief in the moonlight, then obviously the thief would be able to see me as well.

With this thought in mind, I stayed in the shadows. I began to climb through the fence into Bobby's paddock.

Suddenly, something grabbed me from behind.

I tried to scream, but only a tiny squeak came out. Looking back, I realized that my attacker was only a fencepost nail. I tried to jiggle my dressing gown free from the nail, but it wouldn't budge.

Not taking my eyes off the shadowy figure near Reese's house, I shrugged out of my dressing gown and left it hanging on the fence. I was so focused that I barely noticed the sudden chill through the thin fabric of my pyjamas.

I crouched low, sticking close to the fence line as I made my way closer to the Moriartys' property.

As I carefully climbed through the fence into Reese's yard, I sought the cover of a half-grown pine tree to hide behind. The shadowy figure disappeared behind the Moriartys' house and then reappeared in the back yard.

The figure slowed, and then came to a stop, looking around. I knew the thief was looking for a horse.

I had one small advantage that could help me to gain some time. I knew where Jefferson was. The thief didn't.

While Bobby stayed out in a paddock both day and night, Reese always put Jefferson in his stable at night. The stable was located behind the Moriartys' shed.

I didn't stop to think about my own safety. All I knew was that I had to get to Jefferson first.

I patted my pocket for my mobile phone, but it was empty. I checked my pocket again, then felt around on the ground. The phone was gone.

Suddenly, I felt more alone than I'd ever felt before.

Two stupid mistakes had led the thief to Jefferson in the first place. First, my stupid mistake. I'd written – and sent – that email. And now the thief had made a stupid mistake. He'd gone to the wrong house.

But how was I going to explain that to Reese? I didn't want to lose a friend or let poor Jefferson lose his tail.

I managed to avoid being seen as I made my way to the stable.

I could see Jefferson's broad grey back over the stable door. He was facing into the stable, chewing hay from a rack in the corner.

Jefferson's beautiful tail – steel grey streaked with white – was pointed towards the door. It would be easy for the thief to steal it. I felt a moment of panic.

All the thief had to do was open the door and reach out to grasp the tail in his hands. He could cut it off Jefferson in seconds.

The figure was moving again, heading towards the stable and Jefferson. I looked around frantically. There must be something I could use to distract the thief.

I almost tripped over something. I looked down and realized that Jonesy had escaped from the laundry room.

I had no time to think about Jonesy. My eyes fell on a pair of buckets just outside the stable door.

The buckets were the ones that Reese used to carry Jefferson's feed and water. I clearly remembered talking to Reese about those buckets not that long ago.

"Metal buckets are much better than plastic ones," Reese had said.

When I had mentioned that they looked heavier than plastic, and therefore harder to manage, Reese shook her head. "Plastic buckets are lighter, that's true. But the metal ones last and last," she had told me. "The plastic cracks and breaks off after a while, but the metal never breaks. Even if a horse accidentally kicks it or something, the worst that can happen is a little dent."

I crouched beside the stable door, huddled in the shadows. The figure was moving in closer to the stable and would soon be close enough to see me.

I noted several details. Laura had been right. The thief was a man. He was very short. Not as old as my parents but a lot older than me. I guessed he was in his late twenties. That meant it wasn't Mr Waltham.

So much for my great detective work, I thought to myself.

I also noticed something else glinting in the man's hand – a steel scissor blade.

I gasped aloud.

The thief stopped moving, then turned slowly towards the sound. I held my breath. I backed away, trying to hide in the shadows.

My foot accidentally tapped against one of the buckets. A loud clang rang out in the quiet. A torch beam suddenly shone brightly right on my face.

"It's just a kid," the man said with a sneer.

A menacing growl came from somewhere to my left. The man shone the torch closer to the ground, eventually landing on Jonesy, standing beside me.

"A kid and a stupid little mutt. Take your dog and go home now, kid, and you won't get hurt," the thief said. Then he edged closer to the stable door.

I acted without thinking. I snapped open the bolt on the stable door and ran in behind Jefferson. With the scissors in front of him, the man ran in after me.

As the thief ran in, Jefferson snorted with alarm and flung his head up. The horse spun around in the box. His eyes rolled back, showing white in the corners.

Jonesy leapt at the man and latched on to one ankle. The thief let out a cry of pain and fell backward. The scissors clattered to the ground with a loud clang.

Jefferson bolted out of the stable. Edging myself around the stable walls and away from the thief, I made my way to the doorway. First, I snatched the scissors from the floor.

Then I picked up a bucket and threw it at the thief, who was trying to get back on his feet. I threw the second bucket, and he got tangled in the buckets. He tried to stand up, but he kept falling back over. The noise was horrendous.

I shrank back in fright as the man caught sight of me and snarled.

"Jonesy, come," I yelled at the dog.

Jonesy released his grip on the man's ankle and ran to me. The man tried to get back up, but his foot caught in the metal handle of a bucket.

I closed the stable door shut. Then I slammed the bolt into its slot.

"Hey, open that door!" the man demanded, pounding on the wood. "Open up!"

I backed quickly away from the stable. Then Jonesy began barking loudly, and a light appeared inside Reese's house, followed by another one.

Suddenly, more torch beams were pointing my way. A policeman appeared, then another. Mrs Moriarty and Reese, both wearing pyjamas, came out of the house. Reese saw that Jefferson was loose in the backyard and went to catch him.

"Annie, shut your dog up," Reese complained, leading Jefferson over to me. "What are you doing here?"

"Where did you come from?" Mrs Moriarty asked one of the policemen.

"And would someone please tell me what's going on?" added Reese.

A policeman opened the stable door and

found the man crouched in a corner. He squinted when the powerful beam of a police torch shone in his face.

My body sank to the ground. My legs and hands trembled. The tail thief had been caught, but I was in more trouble than ever.

Chapter Twelve

The next two weeks were filled with a dozen or more lectures from people warning me about taking the law into my own hands.

First, I received a talking-to from the police. Did I realize that I had placed myself in a very dangerous position? Was I aware that I could have been seriously hurt?

Apparently, the police had been tailing the thief. They'd been waiting for a chance to catch him in the act. One of the policemen told me that I had nearly wrecked their entire operation.

Then Mrs Moriarty yelled at me for not coming to wake her up instead of taking on the thief by myself. "What were you thinking, Annie?" she said.

I tried to explain about my mobile phone, which I later found in the pocket of my dressing gown. Mrs Moriarty wasn't impressed.

Reese didn't say anything. Not one word.

That was the worst part. She didn't tell me off, but she also didn't say anything to make me feel better. I knew that she was mad at me.

Even I couldn't come up with any reason why she should forgive me.

My parents took a while to recover from the shock of hearing about the events at Reese's place. They had both slept through the whole thing.

"Annie, why didn't you wake us up?" my mother demanded the next day.

"That was incredibly dangerous, young lady," said my father.

"I was just trying to make everything right," I said. "I was trying to make up for my stupid email mistake."

"I blame myself," my mother said, shaking her head. "We've been so busy lately, we haven't been spending much time together as a family."

"Mum, no –" I began.

"Annie," my father interrupted, "I think maybe your mother is right."

Then I found myself being crushed in a huge bear hug by my father.

"Don't you ever do anything like that again," he muttered.

I gave a shaky laugh and promised. I was grateful I wasn't grounded from riding for even longer. But I knew it wasn't going to be the last discussion my parents had with me about the incident.

* * *

Two weeks later, I strained slightly as I tightened the girth on Bobby's saddle.

Finally, I was allowed to ride again.

I checked that my riding-club uniform was in order and my helmet was securely fastened under my chin. Then I sprang on to Bobby's back and trotted down the drive.

I met Reese at the gate, and we turned our horses in the direction of the country park. The bridle path was a shortcut to the riding club. Reese and I often rode that way together.

Mrs Moriarty would meet us at the club later that day. She would bring grooming equipment, hay for the horses' lunches, and buckets for water.

The last time I had seen Reese was at the police station, where we had been called in to give statements about the tail thief.

Reese still hadn't talked to me about what had happened.

Carefully, I asked, "So ... have you forgiven me yet?"

Reese sniffed. "Would you forgive you if you were in my position?" she asked.

"Yes." My answer was definite. "At least we know our horses are safe again."

"But you put them in direct danger by sending that email," Reese argued. "You put Jefferson in danger. I hate to think what would have happened to him if that thief hadn't been caught."

"I know," I said. "I truly am sorry. It was really dumb of me. But I was trying to help. And I've already been lectured by everybody else."

"Hmmm," Reese murmured.

"And the thief was caught, after all," I continued tentatively. "Thanks partly to Jonesy."

"Ugh! That dog!" Reese complained, rolling her eyes.

"You should have seen him, Reese," I said. "Jonesy turned into a complete guard dog."

"Smallest guard dog I've ever seen," Reese muttered, not sounding impressed.

We rode in silence for a while. Then Reese let out a loud sigh.

"Look, Annie, I know you didn't mean to put Jefferson in danger, and you did save him in the end," she said. "I guess I can forgive you – and the dog."

I grinned in relief. It was good to know that Reese wasn't going to hold a grudge against me anymore.

We arrived at the riding club grounds and joined Jessica, Matt, and Austin for gear check.

Matt and Laura had already called me, anxious to hear the whole story. I could tell Matt was a little disappointed that he hadn't been in on the action.

"Did you hear about Erica?" Matt asked as Reese and I dismounted.

"Yes," I said. "She and Cadence won the dressage competition. It's great advertising for Erica's business."

I had heard about the win the last time I had worked at the stables. Erica had also given me a lecture about how dangerously I had behaved.

I knew, though, that Erica was extremely relieved that the tail thief was going to be locked up. It meant that the horses at her stable were safe again. She wouldn't have to worry about her clients moving their horses anymore.

As always, Jessica was quick to bring the conversation around to herself.

"Ripple and I are entered for next week's show at Glenhope," she interrupted. "It's the first one of the season. I'm sure we're going to win Supreme Champion."

"Don't get so ahead of yourself, Jessica," Reese snapped at her. "You haven't won the sash yet." Reese could never resist a chance to bring Jessica down to earth.

"I really hope you do win, Jessica," I said kindly. Reese stared at me with her mouth open in surprise.

"After all," I continued, "it was Ripple's false tail that first led us to solve the mystery of the tail cutter."

"Um, thanks," said Jessica.

I could see that Jessica wasn't used to me being friendly to her. But I'd had a lot of time to think about things during the two weeks I was grounded.

I decided that it was much easier to be nice to people, even the annoying ones. Jessica couldn't help being a show-off. It just came naturally to her.

I couldn't resist teasing Jessica just a little bit, though. "Maybe Reese and I should take our horses to the show, too," I suggested innocently.

Reese was staring at me as if I had just announced I was going to Antarctica for my summer holidays.

"After all, our Jefferson and Bobby both have such beautifully thick tails," I continued.

Reese finally caught on. "Oh yeah," she added. "Maybe we could win a ribbon or two ourselves. What do you think, Jessica? Is there a ribbon awarded for the most natural-looking tail?"

Jessica glared at both of us. "For your information, I've decided not to buy that false tail after all," she said. "After everything that's happened around here lately, I couldn't stand to look at it."

Reese opened her mouth to say something, but Jessica interrupted her. "Of course, I hope you do realize that most false tails are perfectly legal," she said.

I nodded. "I think you've mentioned that before," I said.

"Of course they are," Austin agreed with a smirk. He and Matt exchanged a look. Both boys had been listening to the conversation with interest.

Across the yard, I could see Mrs Mason walking towards us.

"Where's your tie, Jessica? Isn't it your turn to go first for gear check?" asked Reese.

Jessica gasped and touched the space where her tie should be.

"Oh no. I left it in the car," she said, sounding panicky. "I have to go get it. I can't go first. Annie, can you go first, please? You know how crabby Mrs Mason can get."

"I'll tell you what, Jessica," I said with a smile. I reached into the pocket of my jacket. "I'll flip you for it. Heads or tails?"

About the Author

When she was growing up, Bernadette Kelly desperately wanted her own horse. Although she rode other people's horses, she didn't get one of her own until she was an adult. Many years later, she is still obsessed with horses. Luckily, she lives in the country, where there is plenty of room for her four-legged friends. When she's not writing or working with her horses, Bernadette and her daughter compete at riding club competitions.

Horse Tips from Bernadette

- Make sure your horse always has clean, fresh water available.

- The best and safest way to learn how to ride is with a knowledgeable instructor.

- If you think your horse is injured or sick, call a vet and have your horse checked out.

- Horses are herd animals – that means they're happiest with company, even sheep or goats.

For more, visit Bernadette's website at
www.bernadettekelly.com.au/horses

Glossary

- **broodmare** female horse that is strictly used for breeding

- **dressage** the art of riding and training a horse

- **fetlock** ankle-like joint on a horse's leg between the lower part of the leg and the hoof

- **halter** rope or strap used to lead or tie an animal such as a horse. It fits over the animal's nose and behind its ears

- **jodhpurs** trousers worn for horse riding

- **lecture** scolding that lasts a long time

- **menacing** threatening

- **mutilated** injured or damaged seriously

- **paddock** enclosed area where horses can graze or exercise

- **skittish** easily frightened or excited

- **suspicious** feeling that something is wrong or bad, but there is little or no proof to back up the feeling

Advice from Annie

Dear Annie,

I forgot to help my friend with something important last week, and now she's really mad at me. I'm afraid she won't ever forgive me. What can I do to show her I'm really sorry? How can I get her to forgive me?

Sincerely,

Sorry in Shipton

Dear Sorry in Shipton,

Everyone makes mistakes, and all friends fight sometimes. It doesn't mean your friendship is over. You just need to find a way to show your friend how sorry you are and make it up to her!

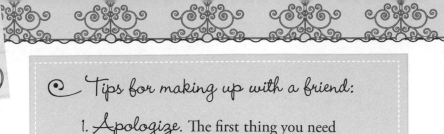

Tips for making up with a friend:

1. *Apologize.* The first thing you need to do is tell your friend you're sorry. She's probably feeling hurt that you forgot about her. (And make sure your apology is sincere. A false apology doesn't mean anything.)

2. *Listen.* Hear your friend out. Listen to what she has to say without making excuses. It's important to understand her feelings before you can make things right again.

3. *Make an effort.* Plan something special to make it up to your friend. If you forgot to do something with her, come up with another way you can help her.

Remember, friendships are special, so it's important to take care of them. Be good to your friends — they're the people who are always there for you!

Love,
♡ Annie

The Ridgeview Book Club Discussion Guide

Use these reading group questions when you and your friends discuss this book.

1. Even though she was trying to help, Annie's email leads to a potentially dangerous situation. Do you think Annie's actions put Bobby and Jefferson in danger? Discuss some other ways Annie could have dealt with her problem.

2. Matt and Laura give Annie some helpful advice when she's in a difficult situation. Have you ever been in a difficult situation and needed a friend's help? Talk about what the situation was and what advice your friend gave you. How did it help you?

3. Jessica Coulson is always bragging about her horse and her fancy gear. Why do you think she acts like this? Discuss some ways you could deal with people who seem like they're always showing off.

The Ridgeview Book Club Journal Prompts

A journal is a private place to record your thoughts and ideas. Use these prompts to get started. If you like, share your writing with your friends.

1. Sometimes friends get in argurments, and it doesn't always matter who's wrong or right. Write about a time you and a friend had a row. What was the cause? How did you resolve the conflict? What are some other ways you could have dealt with the issue?

2. Owning a horse is a big commitment. It takes a lot of time, energy, and money. Write about a commitment you have that you dedicate your time and energy to. What do you like about it? Is there anything difficult about your commitment?

3. Imagine that there is a horse thief causing trouble in your town. Write a paragraph about how you would deal with the situation.

Join the Ridgeview Riding Club!

Read all of Annie's adventures.

RIDGEVIEW RIDING CLUB
If Wishes were Horses
BERNADETTE KELLY

RIDGEVIEW RIDING CLUB
Courage to Ride
BERNADETTE KELLY

RIDGEVIEW RIDING CLUB
Leap of Faith
BERNADETTE KELLY